# CHURCH PEOPLE

## JACQUELINE GREENE

# Dedication and Acknowledgements

First, I give praises and honor to the Holy Spirit for downloading these ideas into me and helping me to put pen to paper or finger to computer keypad. Thank you, sweet Spirit of God.

Next, I thank God for my support system. You know who you are. May Jehovah repay you abundantly for all that you have given to me.

Lastly, God has an excellent sense of humor. He really doesn't mind if you laugh and chuckle every once in a while.

This book is dedicated to all of my church people out there striving to make it into Heaven with a smile on their faces.

Church people, church people, church people, you got to love them and I do!

*Jacqueline Greene*

# Table of Contents

## PART-1

# Table of Contents

## PART-2

# Church People

# Part 1

**JACQUELINE GREENE**

# CHARACTERS:

Pastor Normee DoJudge

First Lady Sallymae DoJudge

Mother Mammy Primrose

Church Secretary/Sister Shaniqua DoFire

Brother Frank Godly

Evangelist Winnie Soul

Sister Trudy Meddlesome

Missionary Mary Stickler

Missionary Clara Priestly

Deacon Chester Moneybucks

Deacon Willis Gossup

Lil mama

Choir Director Lucien Singer

Choir

# SCENE 1

Props: Table and two chairs

Scene opens with Pastor and First Lady having a conversation around the dinner table.

Pastor: I am so tired of church people. (First Lady looks around to see if anyone is in earshot?)

First Lady: Beloved, you really must be careful when you say these things. Suppose someone heard you?

Pastor: And what if they did, dear? I mean it. I am so tired of church people. They are supposed to be the most non-judgmental people on earth, but boy oh boy, don't ever get caught in adultery or do anything they think is wrong. The stones they throw at you, will kill you dead, dead, dead. Dead I say. Deader than dead. I don't think they remember nor care about the commandment, thou shalt not kill.

First Lady: Now, dearest husband of mine, I hear you, but you must really calm yourself down (as she pats him) before your pressure goes sky high and that migraine with your name on it comes back.

Pastor: I am really trying hon bon, but I just can't take church people no more, no more, no more I say! I have had my share and I don't want no more.

First Lady: Now, dearest husband of mine, who has upset your nerves? (As she touches her husband in a loving way)

Pastor: Deacon Willis Gossup is at it again. A deacon! If the leadership can't act right, what should I expect from the congregation. I'll tell you. Absolutely nothing.

First Lady: Oh dear, what did Deacon Gossup do this time? You do know his last name don't you.

Pastor: Even if I didn't know it, the man won't let me forget it with his gossipy ways. Shameful characteristic on a man. Just shameful.

First Lady: So, are you going to tell me what he did?

Pastor: He told Mother Primrose that he heard that Lil mama said that Brother Frank Godly was giving her the eye in church.

First Lady: The eye?

Pastor: Yes, and Mother Primrose came a calling. Pastor DoJudge, Pastor DoJudge, may I have a word with you please (Pastor makes motion with finger in the air)?

First Lady: Poor, poor dear. I am afraid to ask what the Mother said.

Pastor: She told me that I had better settle this matter before the congregation got ahold of this thing and all of the men thought it was okay to give the women the eye since Pastor DoJudge did nothing when Brother Godly was giving Lil mama the eye.

First Lady: Oh my Lord. Was that it?

Pastor: Of course not. We are talking about Mother Primrose. She said that she was afraid that some of the old geezers as well as the young men would seize the opportunity to look her way and knock on her door. So, to prevent any hurt feelings, cause she ain't looking to marry, she wants me to hold a meeting with Brother Godly and she wants to be present as the mother of the church.

First Lady: What are you going to do?

Pastor: What do you mean, what am I going to do? God did not leave Mother Primrose in charge of this church. He left me, Pastor DoJudge in charge of this church. Not Mother Primrose, but me Pastor Dojudge.

First Lady: Alright dear, I understand, but what are you going to do?

Pastor: Your husband ain't no fool Sallymae. I am going to hold that meeting with Brother Godly and Mother Primrose, of course. Immediately.

First Lady: Sounds smart to me, after all, we are talking about Mother Primrose. But honey, you are home now, and you need to take your mind off of church people and put it on the Lord Jesus. Dance with me. Let me help to soothe your mind. Darling, I know that you can handle anything that comes your way with our Jesus. First Lady pulls him up and they dance to Shirley Caesar's " Jesus I Love Calling Your Name" until song disappears and lights dim.

(In church setting, someone can also sing the song as they dance to it).

(If someone sings it, at the end of it— First Lady says)

First Lady: Yes Normee, everything will be alright.

# SCENE 2

(First Lady is kneeling down praying in corner by table or wall)

Music softly playing in the background as she prays:

First Lady: Lord, I thank you for taking the time this morning to hear my prayers. I know you are mighty busy with all of those folks you got up there, down here, and everywhere. Thank you for taking my husband to work and I pray he comes back in a better mood. Lord, my husband is at his wit's end with the church people especially Mother Primrose. Lord, now you know that only You can handle Mother Primrose. The Devil don't even want nothing to do with her, and her own children change direction when they see her coming. Lord, I didn't tell my hubby Normee this last night because it wouldn't have helped matters, but these here church people are TERRIBLE. Why can't they be like other church people who don't give their pastors no problems? Those Catholics don't look like they bother a soul. I just don't know what to do with these church people here.

First Lady stands up and sings "Hear My Cry, Oh Lord,

Attend unto my prayer, from the end of the earth, Will I Cry out to

Thee. When my heart is overwhelmed, Lead me to the Rock, that is higher than I, that is higher than I.  For Thou has been a shelter for me, and a strong tower from the enemy, when my heart is overwhelmed, lead me to the Rock that is higher than I, that is higher than I, that is higher than I, that is higher than I (Repeat song).

First Lady: Dear God, I am trusting that you have already fixed this situation even before I went down on my knees. Amen.

(Lights dim and curtain closes)

# SCENE 3

(Pastor in office shuffling some papers when the door opens and Secretary, Mother Primrose and Brother Godly walk in)

Props: Table, two chairs, office setting. Mother Primrose needs Bible in her hand as she comes into the office.

Secretary DoFire: Pastor, Mother Primrose and Brother Godly are here to see you.

Pastor: Secretary DoFire, you are supposed to announce they are here before you escort them into my office. You tell me that they are here, and I will let you know when I am ready to see them.

Secretary: With all due respect Pastor, but that is not making too much sense to me.

Pastor: Did you say making sense to you? Ha, Ha, Ha. I could probably die holding my breath waiting for something to make sense to you. (Pastor raises his hands and looks up and says) I repent Lord.

Secretary: Pastor, you are so funny. As I was saying, why waste time announcing that they are here when I could use that time to escort them right into your office.

Pastor: Maybe I was in the middle of something, did you ever think about that?

Secretary: (She laughs) With all due respect Pastor, everyone knows that you don't do too much in this office besides shuffle your papers back and forth.

Pastor: Sister DoFire, one day you will push me too far.

Secretary: Pastor, I don't know what you would do without me?

(As she chews and snaps her gum and blows bubbles with gum)

Pastor: I might soon find out. Stop testing your Pastor, he fails the test sometimes.

Secretary: Oh Pastor, you are so funny.

Mother Primrose: Pastor, I don't understand why you put up with that girl?

Pastor: Now Mother, we all need help in one way or another.

Mother Primrose: True that, but some people are beyond help, and I am afraid that you have one of those kinds on your hands.

Pastor: Mother, mother, mother. Let's stick to the matter at hand.

Mother Primrose: Oh yes, Brother Frank Godly.

Brother Godly: How are you, Pastor?

Pastor: Doing fine Brother, how are you?

Brother Godly: I am fine. I was a little surprised to hear that you wanted to see me.

Pastor: Yes, I was surprised too. Brother, how long have you been attending the Sacred, Sanctified, Anointed, Holy Ghost filled, Fire-Baptized, Church of the Saints?

Brother Godly: For about six months now. I attend church services faithfully, I pay my tithes, I usher, I give my offerings, I come to all of the church functions, I stay awake for all of the sermons and I mind my own business unlike some others that I noticed who sit up in the front row with eyes in the front and back of their heads pretending to see what they ain't see and pretending to hear what they ain't heard. Uhumm (clearing his throat). I wasn't talking about you Mother Primrose.

Mother Primrose: Well, I'll be. Let me tell you something you little.

Pastor: Mother, calm down. Let me handle this.

Mother Primrose: You had better before I take this boy to task. You don't mess with no mother of the church and come out alive. Everybody knows that. You better recognize.

Pastor: Mother calm down.

Pastor: Brother Godly, it has come to Mother Primrose's attention that you have been giving Lil Mama the eye.

Brother Godly: The eye?

Pastor: You know the eye (Pastor winks).

Brother Godly: I have not been doing any such thing. Who is spreading such lies about me?

Pastor: I believe Lil Mama told Brother Gossup and he told Mother Primrose.

Brother Godly: That is a lie. So where are my accusers? I have a right to meet with them.

Mother Primrose: The nerve of this man lying to our face. I have a mind to take this Bible and land it upside his head. (Mother raises her Bible)

Pastor: Mother, calm down.

Mother Primrose: I'm trying Pastor, I am really trying. (shaking her feet nervously). I feel my pressure rising to places it shouldn't visit. Lord, help me here.

Pastor: Maybe it will be best if we call Lil Mama and Brother Gossup in so that we can clear up the matter (Secretary DoFire is eavesdropping and before Pastor could call Secretary DoFire, she comes running through the door)

Secretary DoFire: Pastor, you want me to set up a meeting with Lil Mama and Brother Gossup, Mother Primrose and Brother Godly. (She is out of breath)

Pastor: How did you know that? Were you eavesdropping?

Secretary DoFire: No Pastor, the Spirit done told me.

Mother Primrose: Pastor, you must really listen to me on this one, I keep telling you that some kinds just cannot be helped. She appears to be one of those kinds.

Secretary DoFire: It takes one to know one.

Mother Primrose: I don't have time for this nonsense. Can't let these church people kill me. No sirree.

(As Mother gets up to walk out, she says)

Mother Primrose: Just call me when it is time to meet and it had better be soon.

(Brother Godly gets up and shaking his head, he says)

Brother Godly: This is exactly why people don't go to church. This nonsense is unbelievable. Just call me when my accusers are present. (They all exit)

Pastor DoJudge: Why me, oh Lord? (throws hands in air and sits with hand under chin solemnly, he shakes his head back and forth)

Andre Crouch's "Take me Back" starts playing or someone can sing the song. He starts walking around and making motions to God. He sits down and puts his head down. He makes motions to the song.

Pastor: I need your help Lord. These church people are trying to force the old Normee to come out. But Lord, I need you to take me back to the place where I first received you, and I believed in church people, church people, church people.

(Lights dim and curtain closes)

# SCENE 4

Props: Table, chairs, briefcase, book for First Lady, and telephone. Curtain opens and Pastor walks into the house with briefcase and First Lady is sitting at the table reading a book. Pastor goes over and gives her a kiss.

Pastor: Hello, dear.

First Lady: Good day, my love. How did your meeting go today with Mother Primrose and Brother Godly.

Pastor: As best as could be expected. I know someone was praying for me.

First Lady: Yes, dear. That would be me.

Pastor: Thank you dear, but it ain't over yet. I have to schedule another meeting since Brother Godly denies ever giving Sister Lil Mama the eye.

First Lady: I trust that God will handle this situation because we are truly overwhelmed. It is one thing after another with those church people.

Pastor: You ain't telling no lie. This thing is not for beginners. In fact, it seems as if it ain't even for old folks like me. Dear, do you remember how excited I was when I was first called to pastor. (He smiles and laughs ha, ha, ha)

First Lady: Oh yes, Normee. You would run around all day talking about preaching the Word, about saving souls and changing lives. You said you were on a mission from God.

Pastor: Ha, ha, ha. I surely did think that way, many moons ago. Now, I'm not too sure whether it was a mission from God or one straight from the pit of hell.

First Lady: Normee Dojudge!! You had better repent.

Pastor: I repent Lord.

First Lady: Normee, you know church people can be troublesome, but their heart is right.

Pastor: God help us all if their heart is right and they act like that. Imagine if their hearts were wrong, we would all be ten feet under.

First Lady: Normee.

Pastor: Yes, dear. I repent again.

First Lady: Normee, your honey has a special surprise for you.

Pastor: Surprise in the kitchen or surprise in that room back there.

First Lady: In the room back there. (Pointing to the bedroom)

Pastor: Glory be to Jesus. I just love those surprises. Normee is ready baby. Normee is READY.

First Lady: Calm down Normee. You gonna send up your pressure.

Pastor: It's okay, baby. Big Boy Normee's got your number.

Phone rings. Ring a ling. Ring a ling.

Pastor: Let it ring.

First Lady: Normee, it could be an emergency.

Pastor: Why now Jesus, Big Boy Normee wants to see his surprise. (First Lady goes to phone and answers)

First Lady: Praise the Lord!

Secretary DoFire: Praise the Lord, First Lady. How are you?

First Lady: Doing good, Sister DoFire. How are you doing? (Pastor rolls his eyes and is mouthing to wife-Hurry up)

Sister DoFire: I am doing great, praises to Jesus. Is Pastor around?

First Lady: Hold on one moment. (She hands the phone to the Pastor)

Pastor: Hello Sister DoFire, please make this quick, I am in the middle of something over here. (First Lady hits him playfully and says)

First Lady: Normee.

Pastor: Normee nothing. Sister DoFire, please help your pastor out here for once. Make this quick.

Sister DoFire: Pastor, the meeting with Mother Primrose, Lil Mama, Brother Godly and Deacon Gossup is scheduled for tomorrow at 11.

Pastor: Thank you, Sister DoFire. I will be talking to you.

Sister DoFire: Pastor, we have other business to discuss.

Pastor: Sister DoFire, with all due respect, not today. Bless you dear.

Sister DoFire: But Pastor . (Pastor hangs up the phone)

Pastor to First Lady: Now, Big Boy Normee is ready for his surprise. (He claps his hands and pulls his wife's hands towards the room and exclaims)

Pastor: Glory to Jesus! Glory to Jesus! God is good!

Let's Get It On is played or sang by someone as the lights dim and curtain closes.

(Intermission)

# SCENE 5

Props: Secretary will need desk and telephone and Sister Trudy will be elsewhere and will also need cellphone. (Secretary calls Trudy Meddlesome on the phone. Secretary dials and Trudy answers)

Trudy: Hello?

Secretary whispers: Trudy Meddlesome, you will not believe what is going here at the Sacred, Sanctified, Anointed, Holy Ghost filled, Fire-Baptized, Church of the Saints. You will not believe it, I tell you.

Trudy: Talk to me girlfriend. Talk to me. Trudy is all ears.

Secretary: Well, Brother Gossup done told Pastor that Lil Mama done said that Brother Godly keeps giving her the eye and you know Mother Primrose is all in that thing.

Trudy; How in the world did I miss that?

Secretary: I don't know girl, but you are slipping.

Trudy: No way Jose. Trudy Meddlesome don't slip. I get to church early every Sunday morning, I see who goes in and who comes out, I patrol the aisles and see who is looking too long and hard at who, I listen to the words thrown from the pulpit, and look around to see who got hit. I hide in the bathroom stalls and listen to the conversations, everybody reports all of the happenings to me, who talking to who, who not talking to who, who done what, who ain't done what, Trudy Meddlesome don't slip. How in the world did that get by me? Something is amiss here. Hmmm. (She motions and acts as she says the above words)

Secretary: I don't know what to tell you Trudy, but I have to set up a meeting with all of the players in this scandal soon or else Mother Primrose will settle this thing once and for all.

Trudy: She sure is a meddling mother of someone.

Secretary: Anyway Trudy, I just thought you would want to know.

Trudy: Thanks for the heads up, and please let me know when the meeting will take place, so that I can stop by.

Secretary: No problem Trudy, no problem at all.

Trudy: Something is amiss here. Nothing gets by me.

(Trudy sings her version of His Eye is on the Sparrow).

Why should I feel discouraged?

Why should all this mischief come?

When gossip is my portion,

a constant friend is He.

My eye is on the shallow, and I know it's all about me.

My eye is on the shallow, for I know it's all about Trudy.

I sing because I'm Trudy

I sing because I am free

For my eye is on the shallow

And I know it's all about me.

Let not your heart be worried

Every evil word I hear

I am resting on your nosiness

I thrive on your doubts and fears

Through every path you choose

Yes, every step I will see

My eye is on the shallow and I know it's all about me

My eye is on the shallow for I know it's all about Trudy.

I sing because I'm Trudy

I sing because I am free

For my eye is on the shallow

And I know it's all about me

(Refrain is repeated)

Lights dim and curtain closes as Trudy walks away.

# SCENE 6

Props: Will need Bible and flyers for church. Evangelist must know how to dance. Will need additional dancers.

(Evangelist Winnie Soul is outside on the corner witnessing)

Evangelist: The Lord is coming soon. Repent, and be baptized in the name of the Father, Son and Holy Ghost. Jesus is the only way. (She talks to the audience and says, say "Jesus is the only way." After audience says "Jesus is the only way", she goes on to say)

Evangelist: Yep, He is the only way.

(Brother Godly is walking by and Evangelist stops him)

Evangelist: Hey, Brother Godly, how are you doing?

Brother: Not too good today, Evangelist Winnie Soul.

Evangelist: What is the matter, my brother?

Brother: I am thinking of leaving the church.

Evangelist: Why in the world would anyone want to leave the Sacred, Sanctified, Anointed, Holy Ghost filled, Fire- Baptized, Church of the Saints?

Brother Godly: Because someone is saying that Lil Mama told them that I've been giving her the eye?

Evangelist: Must be that deacon--Willis Gossup. That Gossup is nothing but a gossip. He is always saying something that God didn't give to him to say. I have never seen nothing like it. That man can't hold water by keeping his mouth shut, even to save his life.

Brother Godly: I just want to go to church to praise the Lord and to go home. I don't want all of this drama.

Evangelist Winnie Soul: Brother Godly, the devil comes to steal, kill and destroy. He sits right up in church many a time. Sometimes he gets into church people and make them say and do things that they have no business doing or saying. But Brother Godly, it appears as if he is on your tail right now, so take it from Winnie Soul, you just turn your tail around and give him one hard slap. Bam! He don't like that. Or turn around and give him a karate kick, like this (she demonstrates by kicking). He don't like that either. Take it from Winnie Soul. You do them two things, he will leave you alone for a while.

Brother Godly: You are funny, Evangelist Soul.

Evangelist: Funny, but Sis Winnie knows what she is saying. That old Devil used to be after me all of the time because of the work I was doing in winning souls for the Lord. Old Winnie had to learn some new karate moves.

Evangelist-Let me show you some of them.

Evangelist does dancing moves to Waging War-Cee Cee Winans or to similar upbeat song (She does some crazy moves) Other dancers join in.

After song, Evangelist is huffing and puffing and out of breath and she states:

Evangelist: Oh yeah. He don't bother me too much anymore because he knows that I got his number.

Brother Godly: You have encouraged me Evangelist Soul. I am ready to wage war.

Evangelist Soul: Good, Brother Godly, good for you. Let me know if you ever need me to teach you some of my moves. I tell you, these moves are lethal (She does some more moves) Sometimes I even scares myself.

(She laughs as she walks away).

Lights dim and curtain closes.

# SCENE 7

Props: Need choir sign. Deacon Moneybucks will need bottle of water and wad of money. Need three chairs. Secretary DoFire and Missionary Mary Stickler will need phones.

(Scene opens with Choir director directing choir during choir practice)

Choir is singing "Every Praise" (Hezekiah Walker) or other upbeat song. Before song ends, choir director interrupts when they sing "worship in one accord". Repeats that portion with attitude.

Choir Director Lucien Singer: IN one accord. Hold it right there and don't go no further. In one accord my big toe. I got to get this thing off my chest. Some of ya'll stand there and sing the song, and he mimics singing Every Praise, Every Praise, in one accord and, some of you even have the nerve to go into spirit (he makes falling in spirit movement) and need ushering too and then you get up, dust yourself off and go call pastor and tell him how Choir Director Singer don't know what he's doing, how I work you like you getting paid, how this thing is VOLUNTARY and how during choir practice, you can't do this and you can't do that, how I work you all like you're trying to qualify for the Olympics, after all my hard work, this is the thanks I get. Oh my God, (high shrieking voice) I actually think I'm going to cry. Choir break. Choir break!!

Rest of choir disappears, but Missionary Clara Priestly, Missionary Mary Stickler, and Deacon Chester Moneybucks come out of choir and sit around during the break.

Deacon Chester Moneybucks: Oh man, is it me, Missionary Clara Priestly or is Brother Singer overly sensitive today?

Missionary Clara Priestly: He surely is feeling it today, Deacon Chester. You would think that he would be used to it by now. People will always talk, church people included.

Deacon Moneybucks: Missionary Stickler, I wonder who went and started this mess and upset the poor choir director.

Missionary Stickler: I don't know, but they need to stop.

Missionary Priestly: Yeah, especially since this is our 10th director in three months or is it 20? I have lost count.

Deacon Chester: But the Lord was right again, all things will work together for our good , for even in the midst of Brother Singer's pain, I still got to thank the good Lord for this lil choir break. Ha, ha, ha. (as he sips some water) Now, whoever said it, should not have said it, but they not too far off track.

Missionary Priestly: Now Deacon Chester Moneybucks, (laughing) you ain't telling nothing but the truth. After choir practice, I always have to find my bed. Don't you agree, Missionary Stickler?

Missionary Stickler: That you have to find your bed?

Missionary Priestly: Now Missionary, don't be silly. Oh yes, I surely agree. Brother Singer always wears me out. After practice, I am no good to nobody, even myself. I does need a good soaking in some Epsom Salt after this here choir rehearsal. Too tired.

Deacon Chester Moneybucks: Ladies, guess what?

Missionary Stickler: Deacon Moneybucks, you know we don't believe in guessing nothing. Just go ahead and tell us what you have to say.

Deacon: Well, we've been down this road before. Deacon Willis Gossup called me again last night.

Missionary Priestly: Now Deacon Chester, did you answer him this time?

Missionary Stickler: Probably not Clara.

Missionary Priestly: Missionary Clara Priestly to you.

Deacon Moneybucks: I actually did answer him, but only because he called me from Sister Trudy Meddlesome's number.

Missionary Stickler: Trudy. Oh Lord, we in trouble now. Both Trudy and Willis together are nothing, but trouble with a capital T, a capital R, wrapped up into capital O,U,B, L and E.

Missionary Priestly: Let us have an open mind, Missionary Stickler.

Missionary Stickler: Clara Priestly, we're talking bout Trudy and Willis, stop being so holy and righteous and get serious.

Deacon Chester: Mary is right, of course. As much as the Pastor does lay hands on Trudy and Willis, you would think that they would be purer than snow. Instead, those two love gossip and confusion as much as I love counting my money. Lord, help me. (He takes out some money and starts counting)

Mother Priestly: At least you are confessing your sins, Deacon Chester.

Deacon Chester: Ain't that the truth, I have lots more to confess too. You want to hear?

Missionary Stickler: Take your sins to the pastor or tell Jesus, we all got our own sins to bear. Anyway Deacon, I am almost afraid to ask you about what they wanted.

Deacon Chester: They wanted to know if I heard about Brother Godly and Lil Mama.

Missionary Priestly: What about them?

Deacon Chester: Apparently, Lil Mama told Brother Gossup that Brother Godly keeps giving her the eye in church and she can't concentrate on the sermon. She is so taken aback.

Missionary Stickler: Any excuse not to concentrate on Pastor's sermon. Who told you that? Trudy or Willis?

Deacon: Trudy. Why?

Missionary Sticker: They both like to weave tales but Trudy seems to hear more of what nobody is saying.

Deacon: There is going to be a meeting with Lil Mama, Brother Godly, Pastor and Mother Primrose.

Both missionaries scream at same time: Mother Primrose.

Deacon: Yes, the one and only, Mother Primrose.

Missionary Priestly: Oh Lord, here we go again. Remember what she did to Sister Allclear's husband. She accused the man of snoring through Pastor DoJudge's sermons. Now you know, you can do many things to Pastor, but don't dare fall asleep on his sermon, and then you gonna snore too. Even if Pastor was inclined to forgive the man, it was all over when Mother Primrose got involved. The poor man could not get any peace when it was sermon time. Her eyes, ears and camera phone were constantly aimed at the poor man. The only way that the brother could get any peace or SLEEP during church was to resign his membership.

Deacon: Yes Lord. You telling the truth Clara. Remember the meeting with Pastor where Mother Primrose pulled out her phone and showed us the video with Brother Allclear's mouth all open, ready for the fly to jump in. I thought Pastor was going to have a conniption when he saw the video and heard the snoring.

Mother Stickler: Yeah, but for weeks, we couldn't get any peace. We were constantly under surveillance. Pastor would walk off the pulpit and come around each of us to make sure we weren't sleeping. I never drank so much coffee in the morning time before coming to church in my life.

Missionary Priestly: And for months, he kept asking us whether we thought his sermons were boring. That was a trying time. Trying time indeed.

Deacon: I don't know how we survived. I don't know about you, but I cannot go through another one of those situations cause I'm not sure I'm going to make it this time. For I does catch my lil wink or two every now and then during his sermons.

Missionary Priestly: You too much Deacon Chester, too much indeed. Now, what in the world can we do to help poor Brother Godly. I do like the brother.

Missionary Stickler: Me too, but we can't have him going around giving women the eye. Soon the women will feel uncomfortable and stop coming to church.

Missionary Priestly: I think we should give him the benefit of the doubt and hear his side and I also think that we should attend that meeting so that we can try to stop Mother Primrose from taking the situation to an unnecessary level.

Deacon: I agree.

Missionary Priestly: How will we know when the meeting will take place.

Missionary Stickler: We just need to tell Sister DoFire that we would like to attend. I'm sure she won't mention it to Pastor because she is after all Sister DoFire. No matter how many times he tells her to let him know about visitors prior to walking them into his office, she still just walks them right in without announcing them.

Deacon: I don't know how Pastor deals with that one.

Missionary Stickler: She sure is one of a kind.

Missionary Priestly: That is exactly what Pastor says. He thanks the good Lord that He only made one of her kind.

Missionary Stickler: Let me call Secretary DoFire now. (She dials the phone)

Secretary DoFire answers the phone: Praise the Lord!

Missionary Stickler: Praise the Lord, Sister DoFire. How are you? This is Missionary Stickler.

Secretary: Hi Missionary Sticker. I am doing good. How are you?

Missionary Stickler: Fine. I was wondering when the meeting with Brother Godly and Lil Mama was going to take place.

Secretary DoFire: News does travel fast up in this place here. They are meeting tomorrow at 11. Are you coming to see the fireworks?

Missionary Stickler: Yes, along with Missionary Priestly and Deacon Chester Moneybucks.

Secretary DoFire: No problem. We will see you at 11. Have a good day.

Missionary Stickler: You do the same.

Missionary Stickler: The meeting is tomorrow at 11. I will meet you both there. We must pray. And now it's time to get back to choir rehearsal. Lord Jesus, help us with this choir director.

(They all stand up laughing and leave)

Upbeat song is playing and then song fades out and lights dim and curtain closes.

# SCENE 8

Props: Need mirror, table or chair in corner and Ipad to play song.

(Scene opens with Mother Primrose kneeling down praying)

Mother Primrose: Dear God, Mother Primrose here. You know, your dearest maidservant, the one in charge of the Sacred, Sanctified, Anointed, Holy Ghost filled, Fire Baptized, Church of the Saints. I am on duty as usual—specially since Pastor Dojudge don't rightly know what he doing. Dear God, I thank you in advance for fixing that old Brother Godly. He deserves it Lord, make sure you give it to him good. Make him feel that thing, so he don't do it again. How could he think he could come up into my territory and give somebody the eye? Next thing you know, they be looking at me. Dear God, you know Mother Primrose still gots it (as she gets up to admire herself in the mirror), but don't need no young man trying to take it from me now. Thoughts alone would give me a heart attack. Ha, ha, ha. Forgive me Lord. But I really do need your help. Lord, you know when the Devil comes up gainst me, I like to get my groove on. Let Mother

Primrose sit back and play her song. Which one shall I choose. Oh yes, here it is.

(No Weapon formed against me or similar song starts to play, and she dances. At the end of the song, Mother says)

Mother Primrose: That's what I'm talking bout Lord. It just won't work. That old Devil must have forgotten my name. I will remind him tomorrow about who I's be. The Mother and protector of the Sacred, Sanctified, Anointed, Holy Ghost filled, Fire Baptized, Church of the Saints. That's who I's be Devil, that's who I's be!

(Lights dim, curtain closes)

# SCENE 9

Props: Need Papers to shuffle, desk, table, chairs, mother's stick.

Pastor DoJudge is sitting at his desk shuffling papers when Brother Gossup, Missionary Stickler, Missionary Priestly, Deacon Moneybucks, Brother Godly, Sister Trudy Meddlestome, Mother Primrose and Lil Mama enter along with Secretary DoFire. Secretary DoFire opens the door and Pastor looks up.

Secretary DoFire: Pastor, you have some visitors.

Pastor DoJudge: Secretary DoFire,

Secretary Dofire: Yes Pastor.

(Pastor obviously agitated and shaking his head)

Pastor: You know what never mind. (He looks up and says)

Lord, I keep asking for your help on this one. Jesus, Jesus, Jesus.

Mother Primrose: Pastor, why are all of these parishioners present for this meeting?

Deacon Moneybucks: Because we don't want you to do to Brother Godly what you did to poor Brother Allclear.

Mother Primrose: What in the world did I do to Brother Allclear? The man was snoring every time Pastor opened his mouth. Nobody could hear the sermon to determine whether it was worth listening to.

Pastor: Did she say worth listening to?

Mother Primrose: Just a little joke Pastor. Please don't go round now asking us every minute about your lil sermons.

Pastor: Missionary Priestly, what is the problem with my sermons?

Missonary Priestly: No problem pastor, no problem at all.

Trudy Meddlesome: Pastor, I'll tell you! Some people say that your sermons are as dry as the Sahara Desert.

Pastor: Did she say dry? They call the living word, dry. They call the everlasting spring dry, they call my sermon DRY like the desert, dry like a piece of TOAST. You know how many hours I spend laboring in the Word to bring you all some insight, some knowledge and something from the Father.

Trudy: Calm down Pastor, you know church folk don't mean nothing by it. They ain't got no good sense sometimes. Maybe less hours laboring will help your sermons some.

Pastor: I rebuke you in the name of Jesus. The Devil is a liar.

Sister Trudy Meddlesome: You asked me Pastor.

Pastor: I don't recall asking you nothing. I asked Missionary Priestly.

Sister Trudy: No need to get all defensive and hostile. I was only trying to help a situation. No need to go rebuking a sister.

Brother Gossup: Pastor, some people can handle the dryness better than others. Poor Brother Allclear just couldn't handle it.

Deacon Moneybucks: The brother was handling it just fine in his own way before certain people interfered and caused the man to leave the church. His snoring wasn't bothering nobody except you know who over there (Pointing to Mother Primrose)

Mother Primrose: You know who over where? (looking around) You can't possibly be talking bout me you lil penny counter.

Pastor: Now, now, let us behave ourselves in the sight of God. Getting back to the sermons

Deacon Moneybucks: Oh Lord, here we go again. Thanks a lot Trudy. They don't call you Meddlesome for nothing.

Brother Gossup: Stop picking on Trudy, she only saying what others are thinking and she sure didn't make Brother Allclear resign membership from this here church.

Missionary Priestly: That is why I always say, when you see something that you think is wrong, just pray instead of interfering because by interfering you just end up making the situation worse. Can't nobody fix a problem like God.

Secretary DoFire: You are sure right on that one sister.

Mother Primrose: Don't you have work to do?

Secretary DoFire: Don't you mess with me this morning? I haven't had time to put on the good Spirit yet, and the bad one is still around. Shaniqua is her name, and everybody knows you don't mess with no Shaniqua.

Pastor: Okay Sister DoFire. I will take it from here.

Secretary DoFire: Call me if you need me Pastor because some of these folk need some attending to.

Pastor: Alright folks, why have you all decided to show up here at this time? I thought I was having a meeting with four people— Mother Primrose, Brother Godly, Deacon Gossup and Lil Mama.

Missionary Priestly: Pastor, we wanted to help with the situation.

Deacon Moneybucks: For we know how Mother Primrose can get.

Mother Primrose: Pastor, he is really trying it, trying my patience. I know about long-suffering and self-control, but I am about to lose it in a minute on this knucklehead who don't have a dime to his name, calling himself Moneybucks. Ha.

Pastor: Alright everyone, let us focus on the matter at hand.

Pastor: Lil Mama, it has come to my attention that you told, a certain unnamed person, who told another person who then told me that you said that Brother Godly has been giving you the eye.

Lil Mama: (West Indian accent): Yes, he has been giving me the "hi."

Pastor: Now Brother Godly, what do you have to say for yourself?

Brother Godly: I have been giving you the eye Lil Mama?

Lil Mama: Of course, every time may meet you, you give me the "hi."

Mother Primrose: I told you Pastor, I told you. This must stop in the name of Jesus. This eye business cannot continue here at the Sacred, Sanctified, Anointed, Holy Ghost filled, Fire Baptized, Church of the Saints. No way Jose, you have picked the wrong church this time buddy.

Missionary Priestly: Hold on one minute, let us not be too quick to judge this situation.

Mother Primrose: Who is judging? Everybody knows that the Bible says thou shalt not judge. Everybody knows that! You talking like you schooling somebody on something.

Mother Primrose: (under her breath): But I knows that I was right. Nobody can pull one over on the mother of this church. The Devil can't hide here. Nosireee.

Lil Mama: Pastor, what is all of the fuss over Brother Godly giving me the "hi".

Mother Primrose: Lord have mercy chile, we have got to get you into some deliverance.

Brother Godly: Sister Lil Mama, I have always been good to you. I don't know why you have decided to slander my good name. But I have some moves for you.

Mother Primrose: Oh Lord Jesus, this man has lost his mind. He is going to show his moves to the young lady in this house of the Lord, this Sacred, Sanctified, Anointed, Holy Ghost filled, Fire-Baptized Church of the Saints and in front of all of us. Lord, my heart can't take this. Pastor DoJudge, WHAT DO YOU HAVE TO SAY?

Pastor DoJudge: Let us be calm.

Mother Primrose: Pastor, I am sick of all of this talking. All you ever do is try to bring peace to every situation when sometimes you have to put your foot down.

Deacon Moneybucks: I know where I would like to put my foot, Pastor. Yessiree. I know the spot exactly. Just give me the word Pastor.

Pastor: Sister Lil Mama, are you feeling uncomfortable when Brother Godly gives you the eye?

Brother Gossup: Yes, Sister Lil Mama. Tell the Pastor. Don't be scared.

Lil Mama: No Pastor. It feels kind of nice.

Brother Gossup: Well I'll be.

Mother Primrose: Dear Jesus, dear Jesus, the Devil trying to take up territory in my church. Dear Jesus. 911. Jesus. 911.

Missionary Stickler: Lord, have mercy.

Missionary Priestly: Shh Mary. Don't add fuel to the fire. Lil Mama, what do you mean it feels kind of nice?

Missionary Stickler: Now Clara, has it been so long that you don't know what feel nice means?

Missionary Priestly: Go on chile, don't pay these sinful people no mind. What feels nice about when Brother Godly gives you the eye?

Lil Mama: Well, Missionary Clara, I have been coming to Sacred, Sanctified, Anointed, Holy Ghost filled, Fire Baptized, Church of the Saints for three years now, and Brother Godly is the only one who always gives me the "hi" after service. He stops to talk to me and asks me about my family. He's nice every time.

Pastor: Ok. I think I understand the problem.

Mother Primrose: It's bout time you see the man as the problem.

Pastor: Sorry to say, but this man is not the problem.

Mother Primrose: Say what? Pastor, you gone and bumped your head on that altar again?

Pastor: No, Mother Primrose. I told you once, I told you twice. I never bumped my head on the altar.

Mother Primrose: You sure does act like it sometimes Pastor. Like now, how you going to tell me that this man ain't the problem?

Pastor: There has been a misunderstanding. All Brother Godly has been doing is letting Sister Lil Mama know that he is genuinely interested in her well-being.

Mother Primrose: He is genuinely interested in something all right.

Pastor: Mother!

Mother Primrose: Mother nothing, I been around long enough to know the real deal.

Deacon Moneybucks: You surely been around. We can all agree there. Don't let my daddy tell it from back in the day.

Mother Primrose: You nor your Daddy ain't worth one buck.

Deacon Moneybucks: Oh yes, my daddy loves to talk about you. Ha, ha, ha.

Mother Primrose: Listen, Chest full of No bucks, you really testing me. I done fail many a test in my lifetime and I sure will take pleasure in failing this one by kicking your

Pastor: Stop it Mother.

Mother Primrose: You need to tell him that I ain't playing with too much good sense. His Daddy should have told him that from back in the day. Ask his daddy what happen to his two front teeth. If you gonna tell it, tell it right.

Pastor: I feel like I am dealing with children most of the time. Brother Godly, you are a breath of fresh air. Brother, I say job well done for teaching us all a lesson today.

Brother Godly: What lesson is that, Pastor?

Deacon Moneybucks: Yeah, not to listen to Brother Gossup. (All characters except Brother Gossup and Pastor start laughing)

Brother Gossup: How was I to know she meant he was giving her the "hi" as in hello as opposed to the eye. (He winks)

Lil Mama: Oh now me understand, you thought I was saying that Brother Godly was coming on to me.

Brother Gossup: Zactly.

Lil Mama: Not a ting go so. The man is just plain nice.

Pastor: Not a bad virtue to have in the church. Brother Godly, you have renewed my faith in church people.

Missionary Priestly: Yes, the church needs more Brother Godlys. More people to show the world that true love exists in the church.

Brother Gossup: I think I'll be going now Pastor. My work is done here.

Mother Primrose: I'll say so. I should have never listened to you Gossup. You always telling tales and causing me trouble.

Brother Gossup: You never tell me you don't want to hear it.

Mother Primrose: Of course I got to hear it to decide whether to believe it. My problem is that I always believe it when I hear it. Brother Godly, please forgive me. It is not in my character to destroy someone's reputation.

Deacon Moneybucks: Tell that to Brother Allclear.

Mother Primrose: Pastor, I think I will be going now before I use my piece on this no dime deacon and you have to come and bail me out of the slammer.

Deacon Moneybucks: You wanna bet he leave you there.

Mother Primrose: So help me God. (She picks up her stick and aims it at Moneybucks. Pastor starts to usher her out of the office)

Pastor: We will see you in church on Sunday, Mother.

Mother Primrose: Yes Pastor, God willing, I will be there.

Missionary Priestly, Missionary Stickler, Lil Mama and Brother Godly all get up to leave. Pastor shakes all of their hands.

Pastor: This has been a very interesting time indeed.

Deacon Moneybucks: Time for us to go Pastor. Can't wait to do this again.

Missionary Stickler: I am sure we will be meeting again real soon Pastor.

Pastor DoJudge: I don't doubt that at all Missionary Stickler, I don't doubt that at all.

Missionary Priestly: All is still well at the Sacred, Sanctified, Anointed, Holy Ghost filled, Fire Baptized, Church of the Saints.

Pastor rolls his eyes up in his head and ushers everyone hurriedly out of the office as he states: Everyone take care. I will see you all on Sunday morning, God willing.

He closes the door.

Pastor to God: He holds his head on the back of the door and cries out, Lord, thank you for Brother Godly and using him to teach us something today. It was an eye-opening meeting . Eye opening, not "hi" opening meeting, you get it Lord. Ha, Ha, Ha.

You got to love them. You got to love them. Church people, church people, church people. You got to love them. Shaking his head. Andre Crouch song Take me Back is played or sang as lights dim.

## THE END

Note: Please be careful to observe copyright infringement laws and, if necessary, obtain permission to sing the songs suggested in this play. These songs are only suggestions.

Note: You can also have fun with the characters as they say the name of the church. Since the name is so long, it is okay and comedic if characters omit part of the name as they try to recall the full name of the church.

# Church People

# Part 2

JACQUELINE GREENE

# Characters:

Pastor Normee DoJudge

First Lady Sallymae DoJudge

Mother Mammy Primrose

Sister Shaniqua DoFire

Sister Millennial Jones

Sister Trudy Meddlesome

Brother Willis Gossup

Deacon Chester Moneybucks

Missionary Clara Priestly

Missionary Mary Stickler

Brother Frank Godly

Evangelist Winnie Soul

Three kids

# SCENE 1

**First Lady reading at table. Pastor walks in.**

Pastor: Good evening, hon bon.

First Lady: Good evening, dear. How was your day and how did the meeting go?

Pastor: It went well, Sallymae. The eye business was only a misunderstanding, but we straightened it all out.

First Lady: Great Normee, but what was the misunderstanding.

Pastor: Well Lil Mama was only saying that Brother Godly was nice in that he would always say "**hi**" to her after service and ask her how her family was doing. He was not giving her the **eye** and coming on to her. Somehow it was miscommunicated. I think maybe because of her accent.

First Lady: All of that drama with Mother Primrose because of Lil Mama's accent.

Pastor: Yes ma'am. Can you believe it?

First Lady: Of course I can. We are talking about Mother Primrose. What did the Mother say after the misunderstanding?

Pastor: She apologized to Brother Godly.

First Lady: Mother Primrose apologized?

Pastor: She surely did.

First Lady: Now that is what I call progress. That was the right thing for her to do. I am proud of Mother Primrose. There is hope for her yet.

Pastor: Yes, and Frank Godly restored my faith in church people. I feel like the old Normee again.

First Lady: Happy to hear Normee.

Phone rings. First Lady answers the phone.

First Lady: Hello.

Secretary DoFire: Good day, First Lady. How are you?

First Lady: I am fine, Secretary DoFire. How are you?

Secretary Dofire: I am fine First Lady, is Pastor around?

First Lady: Sure. Honey, it's for you, Secretary DoFire.

Pastor: Not again Lord, I just left the scene, I mean the church. Hello Secretary DoFire.

Secretary DoFire: Good day Pastor. I know you are probably wondering why I am calling you so soon after that insane meeting we just had.

Pastor: It did cross my mind. How may I help you?

Secretary: Mother Primrose just called, and she needs to see you.

Pastor: You have got to be kidding. It hasn't even been twenty minutes since I left that meeting with Mother Primrose and the other parishioners. I am about to spend some time laboring in the Word. Did she say what she wanted?

Secretary: She said that she needs to meet with you tomorrow after church.

Pastor: Okay. Tell her that I will meet with her tomorrow after service.

Secretary: Sure thing, Pastor.

Pastor: Please make sure that I am only meeting with Mother Primrose. Don't need Deacon Gossup and Trudy adding gasoline to this fire she is about to set.

Secretary: Sure thing, Pastor. Have a good night.

Pastor: Good night, Secretary DoFire. I will see you tomorrow.

First Lady: Is everything alright?

Pastor: Of course not. Here we go again Sallymae. It hasn't even been twenty minutes good and Mother Primrose is calling again. I could hear her in my head, finger pointing, Pastor DoJudge, Pastor DoJudge. Not even 20 minutes good. Am I to be tortured every day of my life because of Mother Primrose? Tortured because I answered the Lord's call. Maybe I should have answered the call and said nobody home or wrong number. Better yet, I should have had Siri answer the phone and say unavailable.

First Lady: Normee.

Pastor: Yes dear, I repent. Anyway Sallymae, it is time for me to start laboring in the Word. Honey, do you think my sermons are dry like a piece of toast.

First Lady: No Normee, why?

Pastor: Trudy Meddlesome called my sermons dry as the Sahara Desert. She said less laboring might help my sermons some.

First Lady: Church people and their mouth. Scary combination. I wonder what the Mother wants.

Pastor: Sallymae, I asked you about my sermons.

First Lady: Thanks a lot Trudy. Your sermons are fine, Normee. I wonder what the Mother wants.

Pastor: I don't know Sallymae, but I do know that it is time.

First Lady: Time for what Normee?

Pastor: Time to cry, Sallymae, time to cry.

Pastor sobs and puts head on the table.

(Lights dim and curtain closes)

# SCENE 2

All characters are present in this scene for the church service.

Pastor: And let the church say Amen.

**Deacon Moneybucks is snoring and slumping and falling over in his chair and so is Deacon Gossup. Mother Primrose's camera phone is recording the whole thing.**

Mary Stickler: Wake up, Deacon Chester Moneybucks. Tap Deacon Willis Gossup and wake him up too while you are at it.

**Moneybucks wakes up and wakes Willis up too.**

Musician sings **Let the church say Amen. At the end of the song, Pastor says:**

Pastor: Now may the grace of our Lord Jesus Christ be with us now and forever more. Amen. See you all next week.

Secretary: Pastor, remember the meeting with Mother Primrose.

Pastor: I was hoping that we could all forget that.

Secretary: Pastor.

Pastor: Pastor nothing. I'll be in my office.

Secretary DoFire walks Mother Primrose right into the office.

Pastor: (Shaking head) Secretary DoFire.

Secretary: Yes, Pastor.

Pastor: Never mind.

Secretary: Pastor, why do you always call my name and when I respond , you say never mind.

Pastor: Secretary DoFire, because every time, you know what, never mind.

Secretary DoFire: See what I mean Pastor, you must really get help with that never mind thing you have going on. I'll be right outside the door, if you need me.

Pastor: I need Jesus to deliver me, that's what I need.

Mother Primrose: Good day Pastor.

Pastor: Good day Mother Primrose. How may I be of assistance?

Mother Primrose: First things first Pastor, did you see Deacon Moneybucks, oh how I hate to call that name, and Gossup sleeping through the sermon. I have my camera here to prove it.

Pastor: Yes, I did. Go on Mother.

Mother Primrose: Well, what are you going to do about it? People need to listen to the Word so that it can transform and change their lives. I am reminded of that song—she sings the refrain from the song "**Ancient words ever true**," Changing me and changing you, We have come with open hearts, Oh, let the ancient words impart.

(Pastor shaking his head like I can't believe this)

Pastor: Yes Mother, I remember the song, and what has the Ancient Word taught you?

Mother: It has transformed my life. I am much better now than before I got saved.

Pastor: Really now? How in the world is that possible?

Mother Primrose: Yep, even I, when I look back at those days. I have to confess that I was just too hot to handle. Sizzling. (She shakes her head.)

Pastor: And now?

Mother Primrose: What a wonderful change that has come over me. Remember Tramaine Hawkins' song "Changed". I feel like I can hear it now. **Song "Changed" or similar song plays**. (Mother Primrose motions with song) He changed me Pastor.

Pastor: Changed you? My God. From what?

Mother Primrose: Thank God you don't have to find out.

Pastor: And now?

Mother Primrose: And now, I am just doing the work God has called me to do.

Pastor: It's a calling, is it? Yes, you sure are good at calling Pastor Dojudge. What brings you here today Mother?

Mother Primrose: Few things I wanted to discuss.

Pastor: Go ahead Mother. I'm listening.

Mother: Have you met the new sister Millennial Jones and her three kids. I hear she has 12 but..

Pastor: Mother, that is none of our business and children are a blessing from the Lord.

Mother: So, they say, but I don't believe that. My own children are nothing short of a nightmare. Some children you wish you could send them back and get a refund. Those children that Sister Millennial have needs some home training. It is up to us to lead the children in the right direction. I want us to have a meeting with the sister and her three children.

Pastor: A meeting?

Mother: Yes, a meeting and this situation I have seen with my own eyes. No Trudy, no Gossup this time.

(Secretary runs into office)

Secretary: Pastor, you want me to set up a meeting with Sis Millennial, her three children and Mother Primrose?

Mother: Well I'll be. We can't have a private conversation anymore?

Secretary: What are you saying?

Mother Primrose: I just said it and you repeated it. Pastor, no time for her and her foolishness today. Call me when the meeting is set.

Pastor: Yes mother, I will. (Both Secretary and Mother exit)

Pastor: Why me? Why Normee? Why not Pastor Dominic over there at The Rhema House? He always looks so cool and unbothered. Send Mother over there since he has it so easy. His church people don't give him one ounce of trouble. He could use Mother Primrose over there. Lord, please consider it, ok. Just not fair. Not even 20 minutes after the last meeting and she's at it again. I just don't know what to do with this Mother here. (**Pastor sits with head in his hands looking up to heaven).**

**Somebody sings-Lord I look to you or similarly appropriate song.**

Pastor: Lord, who else can I look to—but you. Please come through.

(Lights dim and curtain closes)

# SCENE 3

Evangelist Winnie Soul opens the scene singing the old hymnal "Leave those burdens, down by the riverside, down by the riverside, down by the riverside, leave those burdens down by the riverside, carry them no more. I ain't gonna carry them no more, carry them no more, carry them no more, I ain't gonna them no more, carry them no more, carry them no more."

As she walks and sings, she sees Sis. Millennial crying.

Evangelist Winnie: Why are you crying Sis Millennial Jones?

Millennial: I got a phone call today from Secretary Dofire saying the Pastor wants to see me.

Winnie: Why would that make you cry?

Millennial: I know what he is going to say. He's going to tell me that my children and I have to leave the Sacred, Anointed, Holy Ghost filled, Fire Baptized, Church of the Saints.

Winnie: Not again. Why do you say that ?

Millennial: It has been our 15th church in 2 months and I know the drill by now. Your kids make too much noise and we can't have them disrupting our church. They are rude and out of order. I try so hard to train my kids the right way, but this new generation they say and do what they want, when they want, and they don't care who they say it to or where. They have no respect.

Winnie: R-E-S-P-E-C-T

Millennial: Huh?

Winnie: Never mind sis. Our Pastor is not like that unless that old Mother Primrose is involved. Daughter, you must learn to fight in the spirit. Old Winnie needs to teach you some of her moves but this time I videotaped it because old Winnie too tired. Video plays with Winnie showing her moves to upbeat song.

Millennial: Evangelist Winnie Soul, you are too funny.

Winnie: Why everybody think I am funny? Ok I am funny, but I speak truth. Those moves you see there are worth learning. When you go into that meeting, remember the moves, I am praying for you and everything is going to be alright. Winnie walks away singing either Leave those burdens down by the riverside, He's a Miracle Working God or other appropriate song.

# SCENE 4

**Secretary dials Trudy and Trudy's phone rings.**

Trudy looks at the phone and says:

Trudy: Lord, should I answer it? It is Secretary DoFire. Lord, I know she's calling me with some news, but Lord I am trying to change my meddling ways. I will not answer. Yes, I will answer. No, I will not. Yes, I will. No, you won't. Hold on. Trudy got this. (Trudy answers phone)

Secretary Dofire: Trudy, what took you so long to answer the phone?

Trudy: I was involved in an internal situation.

Secretary: What?

Trudy: Never mind.

Secretary: What is with this never mind business around this place.

Trudy: What is on your mind?

Secretary: Well, Mother Primrose is at it again.

Trudy: Let me guess, the new sister Millennial and her children.

Secretary: How did you know?

Trudy: I told you that I know of all of the happenings. She is forever wrinkling up her nose every time the kids utter a word or act up. It was only a matter of time. I need to mind my own business and let Pastor handle this one.

Secretary: Trudy, are you for real?

Trudy: Of course not. You know me, I live for the confusion. My name isn't Meddlesome for nothing. I must get involved. Did you tell Gossup? Well, I am sure Mother Primrose already got to him. Am I right?

Secretary: Of course, you are right.

Trudy: Thanks for the heads up. When is the meeting?

Secretary: Tomorrow at 11.

Trudy" Ok. I will be there. See you tomorrow. Hmmm. Lord

(Trudy sings—It's Trudy, it's Trudy, it's Trudy, Oh Lord, standing in the need of prey. It's Trudy, it's Trudy, it's Trudy, Oh Lord, standing in the need of prey (repeat), Not my mother, not my father but it's Trudy Oh Lord, standing in the need of prey, not my brother, not my sister, but it's Trudy Oh Lord, standing in the need of prey. Repeat).

Trudy: Ah yes. Trudy is back in business. That fight inside of me is over and Trudy is back on top.

(Trudy calls Gossup. Gossup answers the phone)

Trudy: Gossup, did you hear the latest?

Gossup: Yes ma'am. When is the meeting?

Trudy: Tomorrow at 11. See you there. I've got my prey.

Gossup: Sweet.

Trudy: But why was I having that internal fight with myself? Am I, Trudy, gaining a conscience? Of course not. Me Trudy. No way.

**She walks off singing: It's Trudy, it's Trudy, it's Trudy, Oh Lord, standing in the need of PRAYER, (Trudy says no, she hits her hand, and says it's PREY not PRAYER) and sings to the end as she walks off. Lights dim.**

# SCENE 5

Scene opens up with Missionary Priestly, Missionary Stickler

and Deacon Moneybucks standing outside talking.

Missionary Mary Stickler: How are you today, Clara Priestly and Deacon Chester Moneybucks?

Moneybucks: I am doing quite fine. And how are you Missionary Mary Stickler?

Missionary Mary: I am doing good, but I have something to tell you both.

Moneybucks: I am not going to like this.

Missionary Clara: I feel it in my bones, not going to like this at all. What is it?

Missionary Mary: Secretary DoFire called me today.

Missionary Clara: Oh boy, what did the confidential secretary have to say?

Moneybucks; Yes, what part of Pastor's business is she telling now?

Mary Stickler: She has to set up a meeting with the new sister Millennial and her three children.

Moneybucks: Here we go again. Let me guess—a meeting with Mother Primrose.

Mary Stickler: The one and only.

Moneybucks: Does that woman ever stop?

Clara Priestly: When is the meeting?

Mary Stickler: Tomorrow at 11.

Clara: Let us pray for the best.

Mary Stickler: Yes, we shall pray. See you both tomorrow at 11.

Moneybucks: See you later ladies. On my way to make mo money, mo money.

**He is laughing and walks off counting his money. Clara and Mary stand there shaking their heads and walk off behind him. Lights dim and curtain closes.**

# SCENE 6

**(Millennial is in the Pastor's office cleaning up)**

Millennial: Dear God, thank you for this job cleaning up the Pastor's office. He was so kind to give me some work when he heard that I lost my job and had all these children to feed. I hope he will be kind tomorrow at that meeting with Mother Primrose. I have heard things about her. What does she want with me? I know. She thinks that my children are rude and out of order. That would be true, but what you gonna do? Can't give them back or can I Lord? I have a few of them that I just might want to exchange. Just kidding Lord, but I know what that meeting is about—these unruly kids of mine. They are worse than BeBe kids and those kids were bad. Did you see the movie? But Lord, if I can't get help from the church and your people, then where can I turn? You said that we should come as we are, well, here we are. Messed up in too many ways to count. I am so tired Lord and I don't know where else to turn. (Millennial's head is on the table as "Take Me to the King is played or sung)

Millennial: Oh Lord, I need your help.

**Knock, Knock.**

Millennial: Who is there?

**(Frank Godly stands by steps close to Trudy's desk)**

Frank Godly. It's me, Frank Godly. Is Pastor around?

Millennial: No. (Millennial goes by step to answer)

Frank Godly: How are you Sister Millennial?

Millennial: Not too good today.

Frank Godly: Why?

Millennial: I am thinking of leaving the Sacred, Sanctified, Anointed, Holy Ghost filled, Fire Baptized, Church of the Saints.

Frank Godly: Oh boy. Here we go again. Now, why would anyone want to leave the Sacred, Sanctified, Anointed, Holy Ghost filled, Fire Baptized, Church of the Saints. Oh, let me guess, Mother Primrose.

Millennial: How did you know?

Brother Godly: I had a similar experience with her just yesterday, but please stay put sister. God will work it out. When is the meeting?

Millennial: How did you know there's going to be a meeting?

Brother Godly: We are talking about Mother Primrose. Her targets change but her tactics remain the same. There is always a meeting.

Millennial: We are meeting tomorrow at 11. Don't you want to know the problem?

Brother Godly: Not really. Just know that no problem is too big for our God.

Millennial: Even fixing Bebe's kids?

Brother Godly: Our God specializes in fixing Bebe's kids and yours too.

Millennial: That is what I like to hear.

Brother Godly: Don't worry sis. I will be there. We are going to wage war.

Millennial: Thank you Brother Godly. You sound like Evangelist Winnie Soul. I will see you tomorrow. Maybe I will be able to stay at the Sacred, Sanctified, Anointed, Holy Ghost filled, Fire Baptized Church of the Saints after all. Just maybe, God has heard my cry.

(Lights dim, curtains close, and scene ends)

# SCENE 7

Scene opens up with Pastor at his desk, shuffling papers back and forth when Secretary DoFire walks in with the entire cast except Winnie and First Lady.

Secretary Do Fire: Pastor, you have visitors.

Pastor: Secretary DoFire.

Secretary: Yes Pastor, I know, never mind.

Pastor: I was going to ask why are all of these people here at this meeting?

Secretary: I invited them to watch the mess up close instead of getting it second hand from me, Trudy or Gossup.

Trudy: Now Secretary DoFire some things need to stay between friends.

Gossup: You are speaking the truth Trudy, speaking the truth.

Mother Primrose: Now Gossup, what in the world do you know about telling the truth? You always getting me into trouble with those tales that you tell.

Gossup: Now mother, you know that you love those tales.

Mother Primrose: (laughs) I do Gossup, I really do, Lord help me.

Pastor: Mother, why are we gathered here today?

Mother Primrose: Pastor, I did not ask for all of these people to come here today. I insist on meeting with only you, Millennial and her three kids. By the way, where are those unruly children?

Millennial: Now Pastor, I will not have her talking about my children to my face.

Moneybucks: That's right. Don't talk about her children. You need to go find your own.

Mother Primrose: Pastor, I beg you to please control your penniless Deacon before I control him for you.

Pastor: Now children, let's behave ourselves. What is on your mind Mother?

Secretary Dofire: Yeah, what is on your mind?

Mother Primrose: Don't you have work to do?

Secretary: I do, but this is far more rewarding.

Mother Primrose: Pastor, half your problems would be solved if you listen to me and Do Fire her. Her name is DoFire, how much clearer do you want the Lord to make it for you —Do Fire Secretary.

Secretary: Fire, why would Pastor fire me? He needs me to keep you in line.

Mother: No more time for you missy. You are shut down.

Secretary: My momma taught me to be kind to my elders, so I will give you a pass on this one Elder.

Pastor: Mother, please let us get to the matter at hand.

Mother: Yes, Sis Millennial and her three children. Pastor, those children won't let me enjoy the sermon. They kick my chair, they pull my hair, they yell, they are mean to one another and they are simply rude.

Pastor: But they are children, Mother.

Mother Primrose: I am aware of that Pastor, but they need some old fashion training or whipping. Nowadays, you can't even discipline your child without the kids threatening to call BCW, ACS or whatever they call themselves these days. Parents need to get back to training these children. My mother used to say children don't rule me, I rule childrens.

Pastor: My goodness Mother, you really do have a point. Nowadays, we give these kids too much freedom. What do you want to eat little Johnny. Years ago, Mama would just put the food on the table, and you had better eat every drop.

Clara: So true. Nowadays, these kids have too many choices and the choices are messing them up.

Stickler: Remember, back in the day, when kids had chores and they had to finish their work before they were allowed to go and play.

Moneybucks: Nowadays, these kids find it hard to even clean their room. Mama used to say cleanliness is next to godliness. Today, everything is ma this, ma that, grandma this, grandma that. It is as if they cannot think for themselves, except for when it comes to being rude. No lessons needed in that dept, in fact, they can teach the class RUDENESS 101.

Gossup: Why are we all ganging up on the kids?

Mother Primrose: Because we want to help them.

Pastor: Mother, I am actually proud of you for wanting to help.

Mother: Yes, I want you to help those children, right out of this church.

Pastor: Mother.

Mother Primrose: Mother nothing, those children are the worse I have ever seen. They just can't be helped.

Trudy: I don't want to add fuel to the fire, but have you ever noticed that when kids are really acting up, these new age parents just sit there in a daze like please God, deliver me from this nightmare. They act like they are too embarrassed or shocked to move. Similar to a deer in headlights.

Moneybucks; That couldn't have been my mother. Boy oh boy, she just had to give you that look, and you would act right or you know what was coming after she got you home and to herself.

Stickler: Yep, your behind was hers. Those mothers did not play. If I ever walked into the house and Momma was singing that old-time hymn—Pass Me Not, Oh Gentle Savior (**Musician sings it, Stickler reminisces as song is sang ) "Savior, savior, hear my humble cry, while on others Thou art calling, Do not pass me by (Twice).**

Stickler: Yes. When I heard her singing that hymn, I knew that I was in big trouble. And when she stressed that humble cry part, I knew that I was in deep doodle. The teacher done called my house or my neighbor complained about something I did! Funny, how she was asking God to hear her humble cry when it was my cry that was just about to reach up to the high heavens.

Deacon Gossup: I sure know what you mean.

Trudy:  Me too. If I ever walked into my house and my momma was singing that old tune " Trust and Obey," for there is no other way (Trudy sings a little) and she was stressing that OBEY part, it was time to start running.

Clara: Some would call that abuse.

Moneybucks: I hope some don't include you. What's wrong with you, Clara? It was not abuse, it worked and we're still here to tell the story.

Deacon Gossup: Amen.

Stickler: Children need to fear somebody, or they will make you fear them.

Moneybucks: Mama would say I brought you into this world and I will take you out and guess what, I believed her. She was no joke.

Brother Godly: So, since we have so much wisdom, we should help Sis. Millennial with her kids instead of banning them from existence.

Mother: We are not banning them from existence. Just banning them from existing in this here church.

Brother Godly: Church is the place where imperfect people come to learn to become perfect, even children. If we can't help the sister and her children, tell me who can.

Pastor: I like how you think Brother Godly. Since we know how we were trained, and we agree that we are the better for it, we should teach our sister those old-time ways.

Mother: Pastor, here you go again trying to bring peace to this situation. Have you ever tried to counsel these millennials or new age parents, they will curse you, your momma, your daddy, and the preacher too.

Gossup: And right in front of the children.

Trudy: Yeah, some of them are even worse than their children. But, Sis. Millennial, you know you got some bad ones on your hands.

Gossup: Yeah, those kids are bad.

Clara: Now Deacon Gossup.

Trudy: Leave Gossup alone. He is only saying what others are thinking.

Pastor: We are here for you sis.

Millennial: You are not going to ask me to leave the Sacred, Sanctified, Anointed, Holy Ghost filled, Fire Baptized, Church of the Saints?

Mother: Yes he is, unless he bumped his head on the altar again.

Pastor: I will not ask you to leave our church. We are here to help you. After all, we are our brother's keeper.

Mother: Brother's keeper? Sometimes you have to know when to let those brothers or sisters go. I feel like this is one of those times.

Pastor: Now Mother.

Mother: Mother! Pastor have you seen how those kids take great delight in tormenting my soul every Sunday.

Millennial: I am sorry about my kids Mother. I will take all of the advice today and use some of those tried and true ways to re-train my children.

Mother: Now we're cooking with gas, now you're talking. First, you can start by telling that bratty one with the braids to stop trying to see what is under my wig. None of her business.

Millennial: I will tell her, Mother.

Mother: And tell that boy of yours to stop kicking my chair to get my attention and raise my pressure.

Millennial: I will tell him, Mother.

Clara: I think I will cook and invite you all over for fellowship just to show the kids that we really care.

Stickler: If cooking ain't your calling, stay out of the kitchen.

Clara: What are you saying?

Stickler: Stay out of the kitchen.

Clara: Well, well, heavens me.

Gossup: Come on Trudy, I think our work here is done.

Trudy: Yes Gossup, time to go. See you all next week, I hope.

Pastor: Don't you people ever go on vacation. Just kidding.

Mother: Yes Pastor, I will be going now. See you on Sunday.

Pastor: Yes Mother. Thanks for working it out with Sis Millennial.

Mother; Of course, Pastor. I am always willing to give anything a try, but if it fails, you know that I will be calling.

Pastor: I don't doubt that at all Mother. See you all on Sunday.

Clara: Devil, you lost again. All is still well at the Sacred, Sanctified, Anointed, Holy Ghost filled, Fire-Baptized, Church of the Saints.

(Pastor shakes hands as everybody exit)

Pastor: Yes Lord, all is still well at the Sacred, Sanctified, Anointed, Holy Ghost filled, Fire Baptized, Church of the Saints--for hopefully the next twenty minutes. Lord help me. Church people, church people, church people, you got to love them.

"Take me Back" by Andre Crouch is played or someone sings it as Pastor exits.

**THE END**

Note: Please be aware of copyright infringement laws and comply accordingly with said laws when playing suggested songs in this play. These songs are only suggestions.

Note: The characters can have fun with name of the church by omitting part of the name for comedic effect.